Mathimaaran's
ROCKET STORY

E. Mathimaaran

© E. Mathimaaran 2023

All rights reserved

All rights reserved by author. No part of this publication may be reproduced, stored in a retrieval system or transmitted in any form or by any means, electronic, mechanical, photocopying, recording or otherwise, without the prior permission of the author.

Although every precaution has been taken to verify the accuracy of the information contained herein, the author and publisher assume no responsibility for any errors or omissions. No liability is assumed for damages that may result from the use of information contained within.

First Published in May 2023

ISBN: 978-93-5741-657-3

BLUEROSE PUBLISHERS
www.BlueRoseONE.com
info@bluerosepublishers.com
+91 8882 898 898

Distributed by: BlueRose, Amazon, Flipkart

ABOUT THE AUTHOR :

The author is a 5-year-old boy. Completes his Kindergarten, his love for space, rocketry, motor vehicles, electronic goods, and his passion to Understanding the mechanism involved has made him think in this direction. This story is a self-made song sung by Master Mathi during his playtime in bed. With required cuts and trims, his voice notes were transcribed into this wonderful book. Every word inked on this book is the words of the Author himself.

AUTHOR TO HIS READERS :

Thank you for choosing this book to enjoy on a magical journey with me. Let's explore every moment of my dream together and discover the wonders that await us with each turn of the page.

E. Mathimaara*

FOREWORD:

Every child will have certain inherent talents, skills & abilities and exhibits them at some point in time.

Master E.Mathimaaran is an intelligent boy. He used to observe each and every objects he comes across and raises queries about the same to the people around him. Whatever toy he plays with like train, car, bus, airplane, television, etc., he would like to know more about them and go on questioning us regarding their use, function, various parts, and different varieties, etc.,

This way Mathimaaran has imagined & fabricated this rocket story which is thought-provoking. Through this simple story, he taught us how to solve a problem by listing out probable causes analyzing available methodologies, and applying a suitable technique.

We have to appreciate his real talent, imagination, and thinking power at this tender age.

Motivating such kids will bring out their inherent talents so that they may Excel in their field of interest in the future.

I wish Master E.Mathimaaran for bright future and also wish him to bring out many more books like this.

J.ARUNAGIRI
ADDL.GENERAL MANAGER / BHEL (RETD)

PREFACE :

I am very glad to be part of this storybook written by Master E Mathimaaran. After having gone through this wonderful story book I got really astonished and dum stuck, that how he understood the TV problem and how he utilized the safety measures and resources around him for a quick recovery.

Through this story, he taught us problems are everywhere and how finding an amicable solution with the available resources, at times of crises and eventualities is what makes one a winner or a loser. This is a winning formula for all situations in life. This is a great motivation for all.
Being a HR professional myself I would like to mention that he recalled the SWOT analysis

I wish Master E.Mathimaaran a bright future and also I would like to wish his parents for their continuous encouragement ...

G.KUMARAGURU
JOINT GENERAL MANAGER (A.A.I)

Mathi was Watching Tv and munching fruits with his friends at home.

Suddenly Tv had a signal problem not able to view any thing.

He was thinking what to do next.

Suddenly he got one idea.

The idea was to refer tv manual.

Is it a connection problem ?

Is it a dish problem ?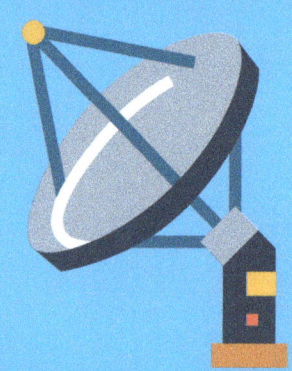

Or is it a Satellite problem ?

Finally, he found out that, there is a problem with the satellite.

Behind the house Mathi has a personal rocket to travel outer-space.

He goes to launch pad in a secret underground tunnel.

All engine tests where done, now the rocket was ready for launch.

He wore his space suit and gets inside the rocket slowly.

Sets satellite as destination before launching the rocket.

Rocket is ready to be launched with the count down.

The count down starts

Rocket launch button was pressed successfully.

TEN
NINE
EIGHT
SEVEN
SIX
FIVE
FOUR
THREE
TWO
ONE
ZERO
TAKE OFF

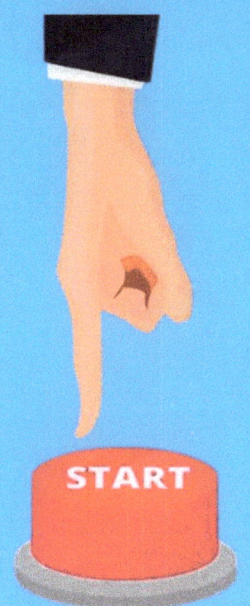

Rocket launched from, Chennai Space station, Tamil Nadu, India.

When rocket goes out of earth's orbit, rocket boosters fall into the Chola's Lake (Indian ocean).

The rocket went into outer space travelling without hitting an asteroid.

He gets out of the space ship, goes near satellite.

With the tool box, he fixed the satellite problem, successfully.

Signal stared to beam from satellite to the dish antenna.

Now the TV is working fine, in Mathi's house.

His friends became thrilled that the TV is working fine, but they don't know who fixed it.

Shares his story to his classmates.

Mathi goes to the school next day happily.

All students and teacher wished for his success. He returns home happily.

Mom asked Mathi are you going to write a book on your exciting space trip, Mathi said: OfCourse mom. She smiled in joy.

When grandParents told this to friends and family, all become surprised an clapped for Master Mathi

Moral : Fortune Favours the Brave

END of the ROCKET Story

CHILD LITERATURE CRAFTED BY MATHIMAARAN.E
(U.K.G-JAN-2023)

SPECIAL THANKS TO:

RECORDING & TRANSCRIPTION	:A.SIDDHARTHAN	M.TECH
GRAPHIC DESIGN & EDITTING	:A.ELAMARAN	BE,MBA
PUBLICIST & COPYEDITOR	:SARASWATHI	MA,B.ED
TYPESETTER & PROOF READ	:UDHAYARANI	B.COM,MBA

www.ingramcontent.com/pod-product-compliance
Lightning Source LLC
LaVergne TN
LVHW070525070526
838199LV00072B/6701